Lily Lemon Blossom

Welcome to Lily's Room

Story by Barbara Miller

Illustrations by Inga Shalvashvili

Lily's room is warm and cozy. Lily's blankets are pink and rosy. Lily's pillows are fluffy and wide, they match the canopy that hangs down the sides.

Lily has beautiful dolls dressed in lace and she has them sitting all over the place.

Lily has a kitten and her name is Josephine. She loves to sit on the window sill just to be seen.

Lily's music box makes a beautiful sound and dancers on top go round and round.

Lily's closet has lovely dresses and shoes. They are of all colors especially pinks and blues.

Her nightstand lamp
is a clown holding
balloons. When she
turns it on it is the
prettiest of rooms.

Lily's room is nice and tidy because she dusts it every Friday.

Lily has a dollhouse
that's roomy inside.
It's the perfect place
for Josephine to hide.

Lily loves to sit in her
pink polka dot chair
and read storybooks to
her bunnies and bears.

At teatime Lily wears a
tiara she made herself
out of ribbons, buttons
and lace from her shelf.

They come dressed in their finest for Lily to see as they nibble on their cookies and sip on their tea.

What a wonderful way
to spend the day with
Lily, Josephine and her
friends at play.

So Lily as we leave you
and your beautiful
room do not forget to
turn off the balloons.

The End

visit Lily at:
www.lilylemonblossom.com

CPSIA information can be obtained
at www.ICGtesting.com
Printed in the USA
LVXC01n1928061213
364138LV00001B/1

* 9 7 8 1 4 7 9 1 4 7 1 0 6 *